From Ink To Impact

Season 1, Volume 1

Mrigendra Bharti

Published by Sellbrochure Vymish Entertainment, 2024.

FROM INK TO IMPACT

First edition. June 22, 2024.

Copyright © 2024 Mrigendra Bharti.

ISBN: 979-8227554123

Written by Mrigendra Bharti.

Table of Contents

Preface

From Ink to Impact:

The written word has always held a powerful allure for me. From childhood tales whispered under the covers to dog-eared novels devoured in stolen moments, stories have transported me to fantastical worlds and ignited a spark of empathy within my soul.

This love for storytelling blossomed into a career in publishing, a world where I have the privilege of witnessing the birth of new narratives. As an editor, I have the unique opportunity to collaborate with talented writers, guiding their words from raw potential to polished prose.

"From Ink to Impact" is a story born from this very experience. It's a tale woven from the threads of interconnected lives, each character grappling with their own dreams, anxieties, and aspirations.

Sarah, a seasoned editor, navigates the ever-evolving world of publishing, championing the power of literary merit. Ben, a shy freshman blossoming into a confident writer, embarks on a journey of self-discovery and artistic expression. Alex, wrestling with his past, finds his voice through advocacy and mentorship. And Maya, a young writer brimming with raw talent, faces the daunting task of transforming her experiences into a story that resonates with the world.

Their paths, though seemingly disparate, intertwine in surprising ways. Each encounter becomes a catalyst for growth, a testament to the enduring power of shared experiences and the ripple effect that a single story can create.

"From Ink to Impact" is an ode to the magic of storytelling, a celebration of the human spirit, and a reminder that words have the power to inspire, connect, and leave a lasting impact.

I invite you to step into this world, to meet these characters at pivotal moments in their lives, and to experience the transformative power of stories that leap from the page and into the hearts of their readers.

Let the journey begin.

Prologue

From Ink to Impact:

The scent of aged paper and leather hung heavy in the air, a familiar embrace that welcomed Sarah into the haven of her local bookstore. Sunlight streamed through the expansive windows, casting a warm glow on the towering shelves overflowing with stories waiting to be discovered.

She wasn't just here to browse. She carried a worn leather satchel, its contents more precious than any first edition. Inside lay a manuscript, its pages filled with a youthful, unpolished voice, brimming with raw talent and vulnerability.

Years ago, Sarah herself had stood on the precipice of publishing dreams, her own manuscript clutched in a similar fashion. Back then, she was a wide-eyed student, adrift in a sea of uncertainty. A chance encounter with a seasoned editor, a woman with a discerning eye and an unwavering belief in the power of storytelling, had changed everything.

Those words of encouragement, the meticulous edits, and the unwavering support had helped Sarah's own story find its way into the world. Now, she held the potential to do the same for someone else.

The name on the manuscript sent a jolt through her – Maya. It was a name that resonated with a distant memory, a face from a bustling book launch many years ago. Back then, Maya was a young woman, shy and yet brimming with passion, her eyes sparkling with the same yearning for artistic expression that Sarah recognized in herself.

As Sarah approached the worn oak desk at the back of the store, a sense of anticipation filled her. This wasn't just about a manuscript; it was about the transformative power of stories, the echoes of change that resonated through generations of writers and readers. It was about the impact a few well-placed words could have on a life, a career, and perhaps, on the world itself.

With a gentle smile, Sarah placed the satchel on the desk. It was time to open a new chapter, to nurture a budding writer, and to witness the ripple effect of a story yet to be told. The journey from ink to impact was about to begin.

Acknowledgement

To my readers:

Thank you for taking the time to embark on this journey with me. I hope you found the story engaging, inspiring, and perhaps even a little thought-provoking. Your support means the world to me.

TO MY FELLOW WRITERS:

I am forever grateful for the community of writers who share my passion for storytelling. Your encouragement, camaraderie, and willingness to share your craft have been invaluable.

TO MY IMAGINATION:

Thank you for being my playground, my escape, and my source of endless inspiration. Without you, this story would not exist.

To the fictional characters:

Thank you for coming to life on the page and for sharing your stories with me. I hope you have found your way into the hearts of my readers.

To the fictional university:

Thank you for providing a setting for our characters' journeys. I hope you have sparked imaginations and inspired dreams of academic pursuits.

TO MY PUBLISHING COMPANY:

Thank you for believing in this story and for helping it reach a wider audience. Your dedication to the craft of publishing is truly appreciated.

And finally, to myself:

Thank you for having the courage to share your voice and for never giving up on your dreams.

A NOTE ABOUT THE CHARACTERS and university:

I understand that the characters and university in this story are fictional. I took the creative liberty of using a fictional university name to avoid any potential issues with real-world institutions. My intention was to create a setting that was both relatable and engaging, without infringing on the rights of any existing organizations.

I hope this clarifies any concerns you may have had. Thank you for your understanding.

WITH HEARTFELT GRATITUDE,
Mrigendra Bharti

About Sellbrochure
Vymish
Entertainment

Sellbrochure Vymish Entertainment, recognized as India's largest book publishing company, has made significant strides in ensuring its extensive collection of books reaches audiences across the global market. This rapid expansion is a testament to the company's dedication to disseminating knowledge and literature far beyond national borders. Central to its success is its affiliation with InkWhirl Media Networks, a reputable entity in the media and publication industry known for its innovative and strategic approaches. Within this network, InkWhirl Publication LLC operates as a vital division, further enhancing the company's capabilities and reach in the international market.

The visionary behind this enterprise is Mrigendra Bharti, the founder of Sellbrochure Vymish Entertainment. His foresight and passion for the literary world have been instrumental in steering the company towards remarkable growth and recognition. Under his leadership, Sellbrochure Vymish Entertainment has not only expanded its catalog but also established a strong presence in both domestic and international markets. Mrigendra Bharti's commitment to excellence and innovation has been a driving force in the company's journey, ensuring that it stays ahead of industry trends and meets the evolving needs of readers worldwide.

Sellbrochure Vymish Entertainment operates under the robust support of its parental organization, Mrigendra Bharti Group InfoTech. This affiliation provides the necessary resources and strategic guidance, enabling the publishing company to undertake ambitious projects and explore new markets. Mrigendra Bharti Group InfoTech's extensive experience in technology and information services has been a valuable asset, allowing Sellbrochure Vymish Entertainment to integrate advanced digital solutions in its operations, thereby enhancing its distribution capabilities and reader engagement.

Through relentless efforts and a commitment to quality, Sellbrochure Vymish Entertainment continues to break barriers and expand the reach of Indian literature globally. The company's diverse portfolio includes a wide range of genres, catering to different age groups and interests, thereby fostering a rich and inclusive reading culture. As it continues to innovate and grow, Sellbrochure Vymish Entertainment remains dedicated to its mission of making literature accessible to all, contributing significantly to the global literary landscape.

Connect With Mrigendra,
Thank you very much for choosing this book.
You can also connect with me on Instagram,
https://www.instagram.com/i_mrigendrabharti.official
With Love,
Mrigendra Bharti

Introduction

From Ink to Impact: A Story of Intertwined Lives and Lasting Words

"From Ink to Impact" is a captivating novel that delves into the world of publishing and the transformative power of storytelling. It follows the interconnected lives of Sarah, a dedicated editor with a passion for nurturing talent; Ben, a blossoming writer grappling with self-doubt; Maya, a young woman brimming with raw talent and yearning for expression; and Alex, an individual who finds purpose in advocating for others.

Sarah's own journey as a writer began with a chance encounter and the support of a wise editor. Now, she seeks to pay that legacy forward, nurturing the potential of aspiring authors like Maya. As Sarah mentors Maya and guides her manuscript towards publication, their paths intertwine with those of Ben and Alex, creating a tapestry of interconnected stories.

Facing Doubt and Finding Strength

Ben, once a shy freshman seeking guidance, has become a confident writer himself. Yet, he grapples with writer's block and the challenges of navigating the literary world. Meanwhile, Alex, through his experiences and personal growth, finds his voice as a mentor, empowering others to embrace their identities.

As each character faces their own challenges and triumphs, their lives unfold in a series of poignant encounters, unexpected connections, and transformative moments. "From Ink to Impact" explores themes of ambition, self-discovery, the importance of mentorship, and the profound impact that stories can have on the world.

WILL MAYA'S STORY FIND its audience? Will Ben overcome his creative struggles? Will Sarah's dedication make a difference? Step into a world where the written word has the power to change lives.

Chapter 1: The Perfect Couple

Amidst the bustling metropolis of New Delhi, nestled in the heart of academia, stood Sellbrochure University, a beacon of knowledge and creativity. Its towering spires and grand architecture reflected the institution's rich history and unwavering commitment to academic excellence. Within its hallowed halls, countless minds had been nurtured, shaped, and empowered to make their mark on the world.

Alex, a bright and ambitious young man, found himself drawn to Sellbrochure University's reputation for fostering intellectual curiosity and personal growth. With a heart brimming with dreams and a mind eager to learn, he stepped onto the university's vibrant campus, ready to embark on a journey of self-discovery and academic exploration.

Alex quickly immersed himself in the university's vibrant academic life, devouring knowledge from esteemed professors and engaging in stimulating discussions with fellow students. His passion for English literature shone through in his insightful essays and captivating presentations, earning him the admiration of his peers and the respect of his instructors.

Beyond his academic pursuits, Alex found solace and companionship in Sarah, a fellow literature student who shared his love for the written word. With her captivating hazel eyes, infectious laughter, and gentle spirit, Sarah was the epitome of grace and intelligence. Their connection was immediate and profound, their souls intertwined by a shared passion for literature and a deep appreciation for each other's intellect and humanity.

Alex and Sarah's love story unfolded like a well-crafted novel, their days filled with shared laughter, intellectual debates, and moments of quiet intimacy. They explored the hidden corners of the university's expansive library, losing themselves in the depths of literary masterpieces and philosophical texts. They spent hours in cozy cafes, their voices hushed so as not to disturb the surrounding patrons, discussing their dreams and aspirations for the future.

Their love was not merely a fleeting infatuation but a profound bond that transcended the superficialities of campus life. They found solace in each other's company, their shared experiences weaving a tapestry of memories that would forever bind them together

Their love story unfolded like a well-crafted novel, their days filled with shared laughter, intellectual debates, and moments of quiet intimacy. They explored the hidden corners of the university's expansive library, losing themselves in the depths of literary masterpieces and philosophical texts. They spent hours in cozy cafes, their voices hushed so as not to disturb the surrounding patrons, discussing their dreams and aspirations for the future.

Their love wasn't merely a fleeting infatuation but a profound bond that transcended the superficialities of campus life. They found solace in each other's company, their shared experiences weaving a tapestry of memories that would forever bind them together.

Despite the picture-perfect facade of their relationship, a subtle undercurrent of tension lurked beneath the surface, particularly when Alex interacted with his close friend, Ben. Ben, with his easy charm and witty banter, possessed a certain magnetism that drew Alex in. Their conversations flowed effortlessly, brimming with shared interests and a camaraderie that extended beyond casual friendship.

Sarah, observant and intuitive, couldn't help but notice the way Alex's gaze lingered a beat too long on Ben, or how his voice seemed to soften a touch when speaking to him. There were moments, fleeting and almost imperceptible, where a brush of hands or a lingering touch sent a shiver down Sarah's spine, a discordant note in the melody of their seemingly perfect love song.

One crisp autumn afternoon, Sarah found herself strolling across campus, lost in thought. As she rounded a corner, her breath hitched in her throat. There, nestled in a secluded alcove, were Alex and Ben, their faces uncomfortably close, a silent exchange of emotions passing between them. Their laughter, tinged with a hint of something more, sent a wave of nausea crashing over Sarah.

In that heart-stopping moment, the truth she'd been dreading to acknowledge crystallized before her very eyes. The connection she shared with Alex, the love they'd nurtured for so long, was built on a foundation of sand. A chilling doubt crept into her heart, leaving a trail of uncertainty and betrayal in its wake.

The image of Alex and Ben, their faces locked in a moment of intimacy, replayed on a loop in Sarah's mind, shattering the illusion of her perfect relationship. She felt a wave of nausea wash over her, the taste of betrayal lingering on her tongue.

Sarah's mind reeled, desperately searching for an explanation. Was this just a harmless act of friendship, or was there something deeper at play? The memory of countless stolen glances and lingering touches between Alex and Ben resurfaced, each instance now imbued with a new, unsettling meaning.

Consumed by a whirlwind of emotions, Sarah knew she couldn't ignore what she had witnessed. The image of Alex and Ben, their faces locked in a moment of intimacy, replayed on a loop in her mind, shattering the illusion of her perfect relationship.

Torn between confronting Alex and seeking solace in denial, Sarah ultimately chose honesty. She couldn't allow the seeds of doubt to fester any longer. With a heart heavy with apprehension, she decided to confront Alex, demanding an explanation for what she had seen.

THE CONFRONTATION

The confrontation was fraught with tension. Sarah, her voice trembling with a mix of hurt and anger, accused Alex of betraying her trust. Alex, caught off guard by her sudden outburst, stammered for an explanation. The truth, a tangled mess of emotions and unspoken desires, clawed its way to the surface.

As Alex spoke, his voice laced with guilt and confusion, a storm raged within him. He grappled with his feelings for Sarah, a love built on shared experiences and deep affection, and the undeniable pull he felt towards Ben, a connection that defied easy definition.

"I...I don't know," Alex confessed, his voice barely a whisper. "I love you, Sarah, I really do. But I can't deny the way I feel about Ben too."

Sarah's heart sank. The words she had dreaded to hear were now out in the open, raw and unfiltered. Her eyes welled up with tears, threatening to spill over. "How could you?" she managed to choke out. "How could you do this to me?"

Alex reached out to touch her hand, but she pulled away, her gaze fixed on the ground. "I'm so sorry, Sarah," he pleaded. "I never meant to hurt you."

Sarah's mind was a whirlwind of conflicting emotions. Love, betrayal, anger, and confusion swirled within her, creating a tempest of turmoil. She couldn't fathom how the man she loved, the man she had entrusted her heart to, could betray her in such a way.

"I need time to think," Sarah finally said, her voice barely above a whisper. She turned and walked away, leaving Alex standing alone, his heart heavy with regret.

THE AFTERMATH

The days that followed were a blur of confusion and heartache for Sarah. She tried to make sense of what had happened, to reconcile the image of the loving, caring Alex she had known with the man who had betrayed her trust.

She sought solace in her friends and family, pouring out her heart to those who cared for her. Their words of comfort and support offered a glimmer of hope amidst the darkness, but the pain of Alex's betrayal lingered, a constant ache in her soul.

Alex, consumed by guilt and remorse, tried to reach out to Sarah, but she kept him at a distance. She needed time to heal, to process the emotional turmoil that had shattered her world.

A NEW REALITY

As the days turned into weeks, Sarah gradually found her footing again. She leaned on her support system, sought professional help, and began to piece together the fragments of her broken heart.

She realized that Alex's actions had not defined her, that her worth was not determined by the choices of another. She rediscovered her strength, her independence, and the resilience that lay dormant within her.

Alex, too, embarked on a journey of self-discovery. He sought guidance from a therapist, exploring the complexities of his sexuality and the impact his actions had on Sarah. He came to terms with his true feelings, accepting that his love for Sarah was not diminished by his attraction to Ben.

A PATH FORWARD

One day, after months of silence, Alex reached out to Sarah once more. He didn't expect forgiveness, only the chance to apologize and express his remorse.

To his surprise, Sarah agreed to meet him. They sat in a quiet cafe, their eyes meeting for the first time since the confrontation.

Alex poured out his heart, his voice filled with sincerity and regret.

Sarah listened, her heart heavy but open. She saw the pain in Alex's eyes, the genuine remorse that gnawed at his soul. And she realized that she couldn't hold onto anger forever.

"I can forgive you, Alex," Sarah said finally, her voice barely above a whisper. "But that doesn't mean I can forget."

Alex's shoulders slumped slightly, relief washing over his features. "I understand," he replied, his gaze fixed on the table between them. "I don't expect you to forget, or to take me back."

A heavy silence descended upon them, thick with unspoken emotions. Sarah knew their relationship could never be the same. The trust they had built, so meticulously and lovingly, lay shattered in pieces.

"What happens now?" she asked, her voice laced with uncertainty.

Alex looked up, his eyes searching hers. "I don't know," he admitted honestly. "Maybe... maybe we can try to be friends again. If you'll let me."

Sarah considered his words. The idea of friendship seemed like a distant possibility, yet the thought of completely severing ties with Alex, the man who had held a significant part of her heart, was equally daunting.

"I... I need time," she said cautiously. "Time to heal, and to figure out what I want."

Alex nodded in understanding. "Of course," he replied.

"Take all the time you need."

***

A NEW CHAPTER

The following weeks were a period of tentative exploration. Sarah and Alex began meeting occasionally for coffee or lunch, their conversations stilted and laced with the remnants of their past.

As they navigated this uncharted territory, a new dynamic began to emerge. They discovered a newfound honesty in their interactions, a willingness to be vulnerable and lay bare their true feelings.

Through their conversations, Sarah gained a deeper understanding of Alex's struggles with his sexuality. She learned that his feelings for her were genuine, but they were intertwined with a complex web of emotions he was only beginning to untangle.

Alex, in turn, witnessed Sarah's strength and resilience. He saw her pain, but also her unwavering determination to move forward. He admired her ability to forgive, even if it was a work in progress.

AN UNFORESEEN CONNECTION

One afternoon, while having lunch with Sarah, Alex mentioned a new friend he had met at a support group for LGBTQ+ individuals. His name was David, and they bonded over their shared experiences and struggles.

A spark of curiosity flickered in Sarah's eyes. "Tell me more about him," she said, genuinely interested.

As Alex spoke about David, his voice animated and filled with a newfound enthusiasm, Sarah noticed a shift in his demeanor. It wasn't the same way he spoke about her, but it held a hint of something hopeful, something genuine.

For the first time since their relationship ended, Sarah felt a pang of something akin to jealousy. Not a possessive jealousy, but a recognition that Alex might be moving on, finding happiness outside of their relationship.

THE ROAD AHEAD

As Chapter 1 concludes, Sarah and Alex stand at a crossroads. Their once idyllic relationship has crumbled, leaving behind a trail of heartbreak and uncertainty. Yet, amidst the wreckage, a fragile thread of friendship has begun to take root.

They both face a journey of self-discovery – Sarah grappling with the aftermath of betrayal and redefining her expectations of love, and Alex navigating the complexities of his sexuality and forging new connections.

Whether their paths will continue to intersect or diverge into uncharted territories remains to be seen. But one thing is certain – their story, though fractured, is far from over.

The revelation left them both reeling, the future of their relationship hanging precariously in the balance. Alex, burdened by the weight of his secret, wrestled with his internal conflict. Sarah, heartbroken and disillusioned, questioned everything she thought she knew about love and trust.

ALEX'S INTERNAL STRUGGLE

Alex's mind was a whirlwind of conflicting emotions. He loved Sarah deeply, her presence in his life a constant source of joy and comfort. Yet, he couldn't deny the undeniable pull he felt towards Ben. The connection they shared was electric, a spark that ignited a fire within him.

He grappled with the guilt of his betrayal, the weight of his secret crushing him. He had hurt Sarah, the woman he cherished, and the pain in her eyes was a constant reminder of his transgression.

Alex's internal conflict was further complicated by his own insecurities and self-doubt. He questioned his worth, wondering if he was capable of true love, if he was destined to hurt those he cared about.

He sought solace in Ben's presence, finding comfort in their shared understanding and the absence of judgment. Ben listened without judgment, offering support and encouragement as Alex navigated the tumultuous waters of his emotions.

Sarah's Search for Understanding

Sarah, consumed by the pain of betrayal, sought answers in the depths of her own heart. She tried to reconcile the image of the loving, caring Alex she had known with the man who had hidden a part of himself from her.

She questioned her own judgment, wondering if she had missed the signs, if she had been blind to the truth all along. The doubts gnawed at her, casting a shadow over her once-cherished memories.

In her search for understanding, Sarah reached out to her closest friends, seeking their insights and perspectives. She found solace in their empathy and support, their words offering a glimmer of hope amidst the darkness.

One evening, as Sarah sat with her friends, sharing her thoughts and fears, one of them posed a question that struck a chord within her: "What if Alex's secret doesn't change the core of who he is? What if his love for you is genuine, even if it's complicated by his feelings for Ben?"

The question hung in the air, challenging Sarah's assumptions and forcing her to confront her own biases. She had always viewed love as a simple, straightforward concept, but now she realized that it was far more complex, multifaceted, and capable of encompassing a multitude of emotions.

A NEW PERSPECTIVE

Sarah's mind began to shift, her perspective evolving as she delved deeper into the complexities of love and relationships. She realized that judging Alex solely on the basis of his secret was unfair, that he was more than just the sum of his actions.

She started to see Alex through a new lens, acknowledging his vulnerability, his struggles with self-acceptance, and his genuine desire to be loved and accepted for who he was.

This new perspective didn't erase the pain of betrayal, but it did soften its edges, allowing Sarah to begin the process of forgiveness. She recognized that forgiveness wasn't about condoning Alex's actions, but about releasing herself from the chains of anger and resentment that bound her.

A TENTATIVE STEP

With a newfound understanding and a heart cautiously open, Sarah decided to reach out to Alex. She wasn't ready to forget what had happened, but she was willing to listen, to understand, and to see if they could find a way to move forward together.

She called Alex, her voice trembling slightly as she asked him to meet her at their favorite cafe. He agreed, his heart filled with a mixture of hope and trepidation.

As they sat across from each other, their eyes met, a silent conversation passing between them. The weight of their past hung heavy in the air, but there was also a glimmer of hope, a possibility of reconciliation.

Sarah spoke first, her voice soft and measured. She expressed her pain, her confusion, and her desire to understand. Alex listened intently, his heart aching with remorse.

When Sarah finished speaking, Alex took his turn, his voice filled with honesty and vulnerability. He shared his struggles with his sexuality, his fear of rejection, and his deep love for Sarah.

As they spoke, a fragile bridge began to form between them, a bridge built on honesty, vulnerability, and a shared desire to heal. The path ahead was uncertain, but they had taken the first tentative step towards rebuilding their connection.

The cafe lights cast a warm glow on Sarah and Alex's faces, their expressions a mixture of vulnerability and hesitant hope. The air crackled with unspoken emotions as they tentatively navigated the aftermath of Sarah's confession and Alex's apology.

"I can forgive you, Alex," Sarah said finally, her voice barely a whisper. "But that doesn't mean I can forget."

Alex's shoulders slumped slightly, relief washing over his features. "I understand," he replied, his gaze fixed on the table between them. "I don't expect you to forget, or to take me back."

A heavy silence descended upon them, thick with the weight of their fractured relationship. Sarah knew they could never return to the idyllic world they once inhabited. The trust, so meticulously built, lay shattered in pieces.

"What happens now?" she asked, her voice laced with uncertainty.

Alex looked up, his eyes searching hers. "I don't know," he admitted honestly. "Maybe... maybe we can try to be friends again. If you'll let me."

Sarah considered his words. The idea of friendship seemed like a distant possibility, yet the thought of completely severing ties with Alex, the man who had held a significant part of her heart, was equally daunting.

"I... I need time," she said cautiously. "Time to heal, and to figure out what I want."

Alex nodded in understanding. "Of course," he replied. "Take all the time you need."

⁂

A SHIFTING LANDSCAPE

The following weeks were a period of tentative exploration. Sarah and Alex began meeting occasionally for coffee or lunch, their conversations stilted and laced with the remnants of their past.

As they navigated this uncharted territory, a new dynamic began to emerge. They discovered a newfound honesty in their interactions, a willingness to be vulnerable and lay bare their true feelings.

Through their conversations, Sarah gained a deeper understanding of Alex's struggles with his sexuality. She learned that his feelings for her were genuine, but they were intertwined with a complex web of emotions he was only beginning to untangle.

Alex, in turn, witnessed Sarah's strength and resilience. He saw her pain, but also her unwavering determination to move forward. He admired her ability to forgive, even if it was a work in progress.

AN UNFORESEEN CONNECTION

One afternoon, while having lunch with Sarah, Alex mentioned a new friend he had met at a support group for LGBTQ+ individuals. His name was David, and they bonded over their shared experiences and struggles.

A spark of curiosity flickered in Sarah's eyes. "Tell me more about him," she said, genuinely interested.

As Alex spoke about David, his voice animated and filled with a newfound enthusiasm, Sarah noticed a shift in his demeanor. It wasn't the same way he spoke about her, but it held a hint of something hopeful, something genuine.

For the first time since their relationship ended, Sarah felt a pang of something akin to jealousy. Not a possessive jealousy, but a recognition that Alex might be moving on, finding happiness outside of their relationship.

AN UNCERTAIN FUTURE

As Chapter 1 concludes, Sarah and Alex stand at a crossroads. Their once idyllic relationship has crumbled, leaving behind a trail of heartbreak and uncertainty. Yet, amidst the wreckage, a fragile thread of friendship has begun to take root.

They both face a journey of self-discovery – Sarah grappling with the aftermath of betrayal and redefining her expectations of love, and Alex navigating the complexities of his sexuality and forging new connections.

Whether their paths will continue to intersect or diverge into uncharted territories remains to be seen. But one thing is certain – their story, though fractured, is far from over.

Chapter 2: Shattered Illusion

The crisp autumn air held a distinct chill that mirrored the atmosphere lingering between Sarah and Alex. Weeks had passed since their explosive confrontation, weeks filled with a strained silence and the awkward dance of navigating their newfound roles.

Gone were the stolen glances, the lingering touches, and the whispered secrets exchanged under the cloak of twilight. They moved through the familiar spaces of Sellbrochure University like ghosts of their former selves, forever marked by the truth that had shattered their perfect illusion.

Sarah found solace in the familiar rhythm of her academic pursuits. Burying herself in dense literary texts and passionate classroom debates offered a temporary escape from the turmoil within. Yet, amidst the analysis of poetic metaphors and the dissection of fictional characters, a part of her couldn't help but dissect their own fractured narrative.

The betrayal stung with a persistent ache, a constant reminder of the love she thought she had built, now lying in ruins. Doubts gnawed at her, whispering insidious questions: Had their connection ever been genuine? Was her love blind to the truth all along?

Despite the emotional rollercoaster, Sarah refused to let the heartbreak define her. She reconnected with her closest friends, their laughter and unwavering support providing a much-needed anchor in the storm. Late-night conversations filled with shared experiences and heartfelt advice became her refuge, a safe space to express her vulnerabilities and rebuild her sense of self.

One crisp evening, as Sarah huddled with her friends in their cozy dorm room, the conversation turned to relationships. Sarah, hesitant at first, decided to open up about her experience with Alex.

As she spoke, the raw emotions that had been simmering beneath the surface bubbled to the forefront. Tears welled up in her eyes, blurring her vision as she recounted the betrayal, the confusion, and the lingering pain.

Her friends listened intently, their faces etched with concern and empathy. They offered comforting words, reminding her of her strength and resilience. They shared their own experiences with heartbreak, creating a tapestry of shared vulnerability that eased the burden Sarah carried alone.

"You deserve someone who loves you completely and honestly," one friend declared, her voice firm with conviction. Sarah's heart ached with the truth in those words. The love she had shared with Alex, though genuine in its own way, had been built on a foundation of unspoken truths, a foundation that had crumbled under the weight of his secret.

The conversation with her friends marked a turning point for Sarah. It was a moment of catharsis, a release of pent-up emotions that allowed her to begin the process of healing. As the night wore on, laughter gradually replaced tears, a testament to the enduring power of friendship and the strength found in shared experiences.

ALEX'S INTERNAL STRUGGLE

Alex, meanwhile, grappled with his own internal turmoil. The weight of his secret pressed heavily upon him, casting a shadow over his interactions with Sarah and others. He felt like a fraud, living a life that wasn't fully authentic.

The betrayal of Sarah's trust gnawed at his conscience, a constant reminder of the pain he had caused. He longed for her forgiveness, but he knew that he had to earn it, to prove that he was worthy of her love and respect.

Alex sought solace in the support group for LGBTQ+ individuals he had joined. There, he found a community of people who understood his struggles, who shared his experiences, and who offered him a safe space to be himself.

One evening, at the support group meeting, Alex met David. Their connection was immediate, a spark of understanding and shared experiences igniting between them. David listened without judgment, offering support and encouragement as Alex navigated the complexities of his emotions.

Alex found himself drawn to David's warmth, his kindness, and his genuine acceptance. He felt a sense of comfort and belonging in David's presence, a feeling he hadn't experienced in a long time.

THE PATH AHEAD

As Chapter 2 unfolds, Sarah and Alex stand at a crossroads. Their once idyllic relationship has shattered, leaving behind a trail of heartbreak and uncertainty. Yet, amidst the wreckage, they both embark on journeys of self-discovery, grappling with their own emotions and seeking new connections.

Sarah, determined to heal and rebuild her life, finds solace in her friendships and the pursuit of her academic passions. She begins to question her expectations of love and relationships, opening herself up to the possibility of new connections.

Alex, wrestling with his internal conflict and the guilt of his betrayal, finds support and understanding in the LGBTQ+ support group and his newfound friendship with David. He begins to confront his own insecurities and explore the complexities of his sexuality.

Whether their paths will converge again or diverge into uncharted territories remains to be seen. But one thing is certain – their stories, though fractured, are far from over.

The shared vulnerability with her friends marked a turning point for Sarah. As the days turned into weeks, a newfound resolve began to bloom within her. She realized that wallowing in self-pity wouldn't heal the wounds, wouldn't rewrite the past.

She decided to reclaim her narrative. She delved deeper into her studies, finding solace in the intricacies of literature and the power of language to explore human emotions. She rekindled her passion for creative writing, pouring her experiences into captivating stories.

The creative outlet became her therapy session, a way to express the unsaid, the unspoken emotions swirling within her. As she wrote, a sense of catharsis washed over her, piece by piece rebuilding the shattered fragments of her self-esteem.

Meanwhile, Alex continued his journey of self-discovery within the support group. He found himself drawn to David's honesty and vulnerability. David, in turn, offered a safe space for Alex to explore his sexuality, free from judgment or expectation.

Their conversations flowed effortlessly, filled with shared experiences and a budding sense of camaraderie. David listened patiently as Alex recounted his past relationship with Sarah, his voice laced with regret.

"You deserve to be happy, Alex," David said, his voice gentle yet firm. "And to be loved for who you truly are."

Alex's heart ached with the truth in those words. He knew David was right. He couldn't keep hiding a part of himself, not from himself or from anyone else. He needed to embrace his truth, to live authentically, even if it meant navigating uncharted waters.

However, the thought of completely severing ties with Sarah filled him with a pang of sadness. He cherished the memories they shared, the laughter, the companionship, the love that once bloomed between them.

A TENTATIVE HOPE

As weeks turned into months, a fragile hope began to flicker within Sarah and Alex. They occasionally bumped into each other on campus, exchanging polite smiles and brief conversations. The awkwardness remained, a constant reminder of their past, yet there was also a newfound understanding in their eyes.

One warm afternoon, Sarah found herself wandering through the campus bookstore, lost in a world of fictional characters and unexplored adventures. Suddenly, she felt a familiar presence beside her.

Looking up, she saw Alex, his expression hesitant yet hopeful. "Hey," he said, his voice barely above a whisper.

Sarah surprised herself by offering him a genuine smile. "Hey," she responded, her voice soft.

They stood there for a moment, browsing the shelves in a comfortable silence. Finally, Alex spoke again.

"I miss our talks," he confessed, his voice laced with a hint of vulnerability. "About books, about life."

Sarah's heart skipped a beat. She missed those conversations too, the intellectual sparring, the shared passion for literature. "Maybe we could... grab coffee sometime?" she suggested tentatively.

Alex's face lit up with a genuine smile. "I'd like that," he replied, a flicker of hope dancing in his eyes.

⚜

A NEW DYNAMIC

Their coffee date was a tentative exploration of their newfound dynamic. The awkwardness from their past hadn't completely vanished, but it was overshadowed by a sense of cautious optimism.

They reminisced about their favorite books, debated the merits of different literary genres, and shared their aspirations for the future. As the conversation flowed, a sense of ease settled between them, a reminder of the connection that still existed despite the cracks in their relationship.

Throughout the conversation, Sarah noticed a subtle shift in Alex's demeanor. He seemed lighter, more at peace with himself.

She learned about David, his new friend from the support group, and the positive impact he was having on Alex's life.

A pang of something akin to jealousy flickered within her, a reminder that Alex was moving on, exploring new connections. Yet, it wasn't a possessive jealousy, but rather a recognition and acceptance of the reality that their relationship had irrevocably changed.

UNCERTAIN HORIZONS

As the sun began to set, casting long shadows across the campus grounds, Sarah and Alex realized it was time to part ways. Their meeting wasn't a resolution, nor a promise of a rekindled romance. It was simply a step forward, a tentative attempt to rebuild a connection that had been fractured, albeit on different terms.

The future remained uncertain. Would their friendship blossom into something more? Or would their paths diverge, leading them towards new and unexplored experiences? Only time would tell.

The crisp December air crackled with a nervous energy as Sarah and Alex sat across from each other at their usual cafe. Their coffee date the previous month had been a surprising success, a tentative step towards rebuilding a connection on a new foundation.

Today, however, a different agenda lurked beneath the surface. Sarah had something she needed to say, something that had been weighing heavily on her heart for weeks.

"Alex," she began, her voice barely above a whisper, "there's something I need to tell you."

Alex looked up, his eyes searching hers. A flicker of apprehension crossed his features, a silent question hanging in the air.

Taking a deep breath, Sarah continued. "I read your favorite poetry book the other day, the one you gave me for my birthday."

Alex's expression softened, a hint of nostalgia clouding his eyes. "The one with Rilke's sonnets?"

Sarah nodded. "There was something tucked inside the cover, a poem you wrote for me."

A blush crept up Alex's neck as he shifted uncomfortably in his seat. "I... I forgot about that," he stammered.

Sarah reached into her purse, pulling out a small, worn piece of paper. The poem, penned in Alex's familiar handwriting, spoke of love, devotion, and a future they both envisioned. It was a poignant reminder of a love that had once bloomed, a love now tinged with the bittersweet taste of what could have been.

"It's beautiful," Sarah said, her voice thick with emotion. "But reading it, I realized something."

Tears welled up in her eyes, threatening to spill over. With a trembling hand, she passed the poem across the table.

Alex took the paper, his eyes flitting across the familiar lines. A heavy silence descended upon them as the weight of the past filled the air.

Finally, Alex spoke, his voice hoarse. "What did you realize?"

Sarah wiped a stray tear from her cheek. "That love, true love, isn't about possession or fitting someone into a mold we've created. It's about accepting someone entirely, for who they truly are."

She looked at Alex, her gaze unwavering. "I still care about you, Alex. But I can't love you the way you need to be loved."

A flicker of pain crossed Alex's face, a reflection of the truth Sarah had spoken. He understood her words, the weight of his deception finally hitting him full force.

A NEW CHAPTER

A long silence stretched between them, filled with unspoken apologies, lingering affection, and the bittersweet acceptance of a love that couldn't be.

As the silence stretched on, Sarah reached out and placed a hand on Alex's, a gesture of empathy and understanding.

"I'm happy you have David," she said, her voice soft. "He seems like a good person, someone who can love you for who you truly are."

Alex swallowed hard, a wave of gratitude washing over him. "Thank you, Sarah. That means a lot."

They sat for a while longer, talking about their lives outside of their shared past. Sarah spoke about her upcoming internship at a prestigious literary magazine, a dream opportunity that filled her with excitement. Alex shared stories about his experiences at the LGBTQ+ support group and the growing sense of belonging he felt within that community.

As the sun began to set, casting long shadows across the sidewalk, they both knew it was time to part ways. There were no promises of future meetings, no lingering expectations. This was goodbye, a closure they both needed to move forward.

LIFE GOES ON

The weeks that followed were a period of quiet adjustment. Sarah and Alex no longer occupied the central space in each other's lives. Yet, the lessons learned from their relationship continued to resonate.

Sarah embraced her newfound independence, thriving in her internship and carving out her own path. She continued to date, her experiences shaping her understanding of love and relationships.

Alex, empowered by his newfound self-acceptance, found himself blossoming. He and David grew closer, their friendship deepening with shared experiences and unwavering support.

One day, while browsing the shelves of the campus bookstore, Sarah felt a familiar presence beside her. Turning around, she saw David, a hesitant smile gracing his lips.

"Hi," he said, his voice warm and friendly. "I just saw Alex walk out. He mentioned you might be here."

Sarah felt a flicker of surprise, then a smile bloomed on her face. "Hi, David," she replied. "It's nice to meet you finally."

OPEN DOORS

Their conversation flowed effortlessly, filled with shared literary interests and a comfortable camaraderie. Sarah found herself drawn to David's easygoing nature and his genuine interest in As Sarah and David conversed, a sense of possibility bloomed in the air. They discovered a mutual love for classic science fiction, passionately debating the merits of dystopian novels versus optimistic space adventures.

Their connection wasn't the same intense spark she once shared with Alex, but it was something different - a comfortable warmth, a shared respect for each other's intellect and passions.

As the afternoon wore on, Sarah learned that David was also an aspiring writer, his work focusing on speculative fiction that explored themes of identity and self-discovery. They exchanged business cards, promising to swap stories and offer feedback on each other's work.

When it was time to part ways, there was a lingering sense of wanting to continue the conversation. David offered to walk her back to her dorm, a simple gesture that held a hint of unspoken interest.

As they walked, Sarah couldn't help but compare this moment to her past walks with Alex. The nervous energy, the stolen glances, the feeling of walking on a tightrope of unspoken emotions - all of it felt different with David. There was a comfortable ease, a genuine enjoyment of each other's company unburdened by the weight of a past relationship.

Reaching her dorm, Sarah turned to face David, a smile playing on her lips. "Thanks for the conversation," she said, her voice sincere. "It was really nice meeting you."

David looked into her eyes, his own sparkling with a hint of hope. "Likewise," he replied. "Perhaps we could grab coffee sometime and talk more writing?"

Sarah hesitated for a moment, then a smile bloomed on her face. "I'd like that," she said, a sense of excitement fluttering in her chest.

A NEW BEGINNING

As Sarah watched David walk away, she realized something profound. Her relationship with Alex, while heartbreaking at times, had ultimately led her to this moment. It had taught her valuable lessons about love, self-acceptance, and the importance of letting go.

The future stretched before her, an uncharted territory filled with possibilities. Sarah knew that while the echoes of her past relationship with Alex would always remain, they wouldn't define her. She was ready to embrace new experiences, new connections, and perhaps, a new kind of love on her own terms.

Months slipped by, carrying the weight of change and the promise of new beginnings. Sarah threw herself into her internship at the literary magazine, her days filled with the thrill of editing manuscripts and learning the intricate workings of the publishing world.

Her evenings were a blend of social gatherings with friends, quiet nights spent curled up with a good book, and stolen moments connecting with David. Their coffee dates became a regular occurrence, their conversations delving deeper into personal aspirations and shared dreams.

David's friendship offered a warm sense of belonging, a safe space where Sarah could be her authentic self. With him, she could discuss writing aspirations, debate philosophical questions, and simply enjoy the comfortable ease of being understood.

While a blossoming affection simmered beneath the surface, neither Sarah nor David rushed into defining their relationship. They were both still healing from past experiences, moving at their own pace, savoring the present without expectations.

Alex's life, too, was undergoing a transformation. Embracing his sexuality with newfound confidence, he became a vocal advocate within the LGBTQ+ support group. He shared his story with others, offering support and encouragement to those navigating similar challenges.

His friendship with David continued to grow, their bond strengthening with shared experiences and unwavering support. David became a symbol of acceptance and understanding in Alex's life, a testament to the power of genuine connection.

However, a part of Alex still held a flicker of longing for Sarah. He missed their late-night conversations, the shared passion for literature, and the effortless companionship they once enjoyed.

Yet, he understood the boundaries she had set. He knew forcing a deeper connection would only lead to heartache. He had hurt her deeply, and earning back her trust was a journey he was willing to take, one step at a time.

A Moment of Reflection

One crisp autumn evening, Sarah found herself wandering through the campus grounds, a year after her initial confrontation with Alex. The leaves had begun to turn golden brown, a visual reminder of the passage of time and the changing seasons of life.

As she strolled past the cafe where she and Alex had their first coffee date, a bittersweet memory washed over her. Her journey over the past year had been one of immense personal growth. She had learned to forgive, to let go, and to embrace new possibilities.

Reaching a quiet corner overlooking a small lake, Sarah pulled out her journal, a well-worn companion that held her thoughts and emotions throughout her journey. She dipped her pen in ink and began to write, reflecting on the lessons learned from her relationship with Alex.

"Love," she wrote, her words flowing freely, "is a complex and ever-evolving journey.

It requires honesty, vulnerability, and a willingness to grow alongside the person you love. Sometimes, love means letting go, not because you don't care, but because true love allows the other person to be their most authentic self."

Tears welled up in her eyes as she penned her final thought: "Although our paths diverged, the lessons learned will forever be etched in my heart."

Lost in her introspection, Sarah didn't notice a figure approaching until a familiar voice broke through her reverie.

"Hey, there you are," Alex said, his voice soft and hesitant.

Sarah looked up, startled to see him standing there. A wave of emotions swept over her - surprise, a flicker of lingering affection, and a sense of acceptance.

"Hi, Alex," she replied, her voice calm.

A comfortable silence settled between them as they stood together, watching the sun dip below the horizon, painting the sky in hues of orange and pink.

"I saw you earlier," Alex finally said, his voice laced with a hint of nervousness. "I just wanted to say... I'm happy for you, Sarah. You seem truly happy."

Sarah smiled, a genuine smile that reached her eyes. "Thank you, Alex. I am," she admitted.

They talked for a while, catching up on their lives, sharing updates without dwelling on the past. It wasn't a conversation aimed at rekindling their romance, but rather a peaceful exchange between two people who had once shared a significant chapter in each other's lives.

As darkness began to settle, they both knew it was time to part ways. Alex extended a hand, his gesture one of friendship and respect.

Sarah took his hand, their eyes meeting for a fleeting moment. A silent understanding passed between them, an acknowledgment of the past and the acceptance of where their paths now led.

As Alex walked away, Sarah watched him go, a gentle sigh escaping her lips. The future remained unwritten, a vast canvas filled with possibilities. Sarah didn't know if her relationship with David would blossom into something more, but she was open to the experience.

She turned towards the lake, the reflection of the moon shimmering on its surface. A newfound sense of peace settled within her. She had learned that love wasn't a destination, but a journey filled with unexpected turns, heartbreak, and ultimately, growth.

As Sarah tucked her journal away, a flicker of movement caught her eye. A figure stood a short distance away, leaning against a nearby tree. David, his face illuminated by the moonlight, offered her a warm smile.

"Lost in thought?" he asked, his voice gentle.

Sarah chuckled, a light and carefree sound. "Something like that," she replied.

He gestured towards the lake. "Mind if I join you?"

Sarah shook her head, a smile playing on her lips. "Of course not," she said.

They walked towards the water's edge, their steps falling into a comfortable rhythm. As they stood side-by-side, Sarah noticed a glimmer of hope in David's eyes.

He cleared his throat, then spoke hesitantly. "Sarah, I..." He paused, searching for the right words. "I really enjoy spending time with you. You're smart, funny, and passionate about the things that matter to me."

Sarah's heart fluttered, a mix of excitement and nervousness. "Thank you, David," she said, her voice barely a whisper.

He took a deep breath, finally meeting her gaze. "I was wondering... if you'd like to go on a real date sometime? Not just coffee, but dinner and maybe a movie?"

A smile bloomed on Sarah's face, genuine and radiant. "I'd like that very much," she replied.

Under the gentle glow of the moon, with the promise of a new beginning shimmering on the water's surface, Sarah and David stood there, ready to embark on a new chapter, their paths converging into a future filled with hope and the potential for love.

THE FOLLOWING WEEKS unfolded like a whirlwind for Sarah. Her date with David had been a resounding success. They discovered a shared love for classic foreign films, their laughter echoing through the cozy cafe as they dissected plot twists and debated iconic characters.

As their connection deepened, Sarah found herself drawn to David's kindness, his unwavering support for her writing aspirations, and his genuine interest in her life. He made her feel comfortable, understood, and cherished for who she truly was.

However, navigating a new relationship while still mending the pieces of her past proved to be a delicate dance. Sarah harbored a lingering fondness for Alex, a bittersweet reminder of a love that could have been.

One afternoon, while brainstorming ideas for her writing project, Sarah found herself revisiting her old journals, filled with memories of Alex. Tears welled up in her eyes as she reread a particularly heartfelt poem he had written for her.

Suddenly, her phone buzzed, snapping her out of her reverie. It was a text from Alex, checking in and asking about her upcoming internship interview at the prestigious literary magazine.

A pang of guilt washed over Sarah. Though she and Alex were no longer romantically involved, neglecting to share this important milestone felt wrong. Taking a deep breath, she typed a response, thanking him for his support and updating him on the interview.

Later that evening, as Sarah sat across from David, a delicious plate of pasta growing cold in front of her, she knew she needed to be honest.

"There's something I need to tell you," she began, her voice hesitant.

David looked at her, his brow furrowed with concern. "What is it, Sarah?"

She explained her past relationship with Alex, the initial heartbreak, the journey of healing, and the lingering affection she still held for him. She spoke with vulnerability, laying bare her emotions without judgment.

David listened patiently, his hand resting gently on hers. When she finished, he simply nodded, his understanding radiating through his calm demeanor.

"Love is complicated," he said softly. "It leaves imprints, even when it fades."

Sarah felt a wave of relief wash over her. She was grateful for David's acceptance, for his ability to see her whole, past and present.

The following weeks were marked by a newfound sense of clarity and purpose. Sarah aced her interview at the literary magazine, her passion and talent shining through. David, her biggest cheerleader, celebrated her success with her, his pride evident in his eyes.

Meanwhile, Alex continued on his own path of self-discovery. He became a vocal advocate for LGBTQ+ rights on campus, his story inspiring others to embrace their true selves. He also started dating someone new, a kind and supportive individual who brought a smile back to his face.

Their paths occasionally crossed on campus, their encounters filled with a comfortable ease and a genuine well-wishing for each other's happiness. The shared connection they once had had transformed into a warm friendship, a testament to the enduring power of shared experiences, even when love takes an unexpected turn.

As Chapter 2 concludes, Sarah and David stand at the precipice of a new adventure. Their relationship is still blossoming, a fragile flower nurtured by mutual respect, shared interests, and a deep understanding of each other's past.

Alex, too, embarks on a new chapter, embracing love and acceptance while cherishing the lessons learned from his past relationship with Sarah.

The future remains unwritten, a canvas filled with possibilities. Whether Sarah and David's connection will blossom into a lasting love story, or whether their paths will diverge once more, only time will tell.

However, one thing is certain - they both carry within them the lessons learned from their past relationships, lessons that have made them stronger, more resilient, and open to the possibilities that lie ahead.

Chapter 3: Ripples of Change

A year had passed since Sarah's pivotal conversation with Alex by the lake. The campus bustled with the familiar energy of a new academic year, freshmen navigating their way through unfamiliar buildings, a youthful exuberance filling the air.

Sarah, now a seasoned senior, walked with a newfound confidence. Her internship at the prestigious literary magazine had been a transformative experience, honing her editing skills and nurturing her passion for the written word.

She landed a coveted editorial assistant position at a publishing house, a dream come true that filled her with both excitement and a healthy dose of nervous anticipation.

David remained a constant source of support throughout the year. Their relationship had blossomed into something beautiful, a blend of friendship, intellectual stimulation, and a love that felt comfortable and secure. He celebrated her victories, offered a shoulder to cry on during moments of self-doubt, and championed her writing aspirations with unwavering enthusiasm.

This morning, however, a hint of apprehension mingled with Sarah's excitement. Today was David's coming-out day to his family. He had confided in Sarah weeks ago, sharing his nervousness and his hope for acceptance.

The Weight of Anticipation

Sarah found David waiting for her near their usual coffee hangout. His face, usually radiating warmth and confidence, held a hidden tension.

"Hey," she said, offering him a warm smile. "Ready for the big day?"

David took a deep breath. "As ready as I'll ever be, I guess," he replied, a nervous chuckle escaping his lips. "Thanks for being here with me, Sarah. It means a lot."

Sarah squeezed his hand reassuringly. "Of course I'm here for you. Always."

They sat in comfortable silence, sipping their coffee, the weight of anticipation hanging heavy in the air. As the minutes ticked by, Sarah couldn't help but worry about David's family's reaction. Would they accept him? Would his coming out fracture their relationship?

Just as Sarah's worry began to consume her, David's phone buzzed. He pulled it out, his face unreadable for a moment. Then, a wide smile spread across his features, relief washing over him like a wave.

"It's my mom," he said, his voice filled with emotion. "She just texted to say she loves me no matter what."

Sarah's heart swelled with joy. A wave of relief washed over her, and she offered David a congratulatory hug. Tears welled up in his eyes, a mix of relief and happiness.

"That's amazing, David," she said, her voice sincere. "I'm so happy for you."

David pulled back, a smile gracing his lips. "This is just the beginning," he replied, his voice filled with determination.

Across campus, Alex embarked on a new chapter of his own. With his newfound confidence and openness about his sexuality, he had become a role model for younger LGBTQ+ students.

He was actively involved in the campus LGBTQ+ club, offering support and advice to those navigating their identities. He found himself drawn to mentoring a shy freshman named Ben, who reminded him of himself at that age - filled with self-doubt and yearning for acceptance.

Unexpected Encounters

As fate would have it, Sarah and Alex's paths crossed unexpectedly that afternoon. She was walking through the campus quad, lost in thought, when a familiar voice broke through her reverie.

"Sarah!" Alex called out, a hint of surprise in his voice.

Sarah looked up and saw Alex approaching, a shy smile gracing his lips. It had been months since their last conversation, and a strange sense of normalcy settled over her as they greeted each other.

After a brief exchange of pleasantries, Alex introduced her to Ben, the young man he was mentoring.

"Sarah's an aspiring writer," Alex explained, his voice laced with a hint of pride. "She works at a publishing house now."

Ben's eyes widened with awe. "That's amazing! I love to write too," he admitted shyly.

Sarah saw a spark of potential in Ben's eyes, a reflection of her own youthful aspirations. She smiled warmly at him. "Perhaps I can offer some writing tips sometime," she said, offering encouragement.

A conversation flowed easily between them, fueled by a shared love for writing and storytelling. Sarah found herself impressed by Ben's raw talent and his genuine passion for the craft.

AS THE MONTHS TURNED into years, life's unexpected twists and turns continued to shape the lives of Sarah, David, Alex, and Ben. Sarah's career at the publishing house flourished, her editing skills and keen eye for talent earning her the respect of her colleagues and the admiration of aspiring writers.

David, unwavering in his support, remained her rock, their relationship deepening with each passing year. They shared a love for literature, art, and deep conversations that stretched into the wee hours of the night.

Alex, too, found his path. He graduated with a degree in social work, his passion for advocacy and support for the LGBTQ+ community burning brighter than ever. He worked at a local community center, providing counseling and resources to those struggling with identity, acceptance, and discrimination.

His relationship with Ben blossomed into a deep friendship, filled with mutual respect, shared dreams, and a sense of understanding that transcended the boundaries of age and experience.

Ben, under Sarah's guidance and Alex's encouragement, continued to hone his writing skills. His short stories found their way into literary magazines, his raw talent and unique voice resonating with readers.

He enrolled in a creative writing program at a prestigious university, his passion for storytelling fueling his determination to make his mark on the literary world.

Fate, with its penchant for irony, brought Sarah and Alex together once again. This time, it was at a book launch for a new anthology of short stories, where Ben's work was featured.

Sarah, attending as a representative of the publishing house, spotted Alex across the crowded room. A smile spread across her face as she approached him, the years of shared experiences melting away into a warm sense of familiarity.

"Alex!" she exclaimed, her voice filled with genuine delight. "It's been so long!"

Alex turned, his face lighting up with surprise and pleasure. "Sarah! I can't believe it's you."

They caught up, their conversation flowing effortlessly, reminiscing about old times and sharing updates on their lives. As they talked, Sarah noticed Ben standing a short distance away, his eyes twinkling with a mix of pride and admiration.

In that moment, Sarah realized the profound impact she had had on the lives of those around her. Her passion for writing had not only shaped her own career but had also inspired and nurtured the talent of others.

She had helped Ben find his voice, supported Alex in his journey of self-discovery, and found a deep and lasting love with David.

As the book launch drew to a close, Sarah, Alex, and Ben stood together, a sense of camaraderie and shared passion for storytelling binding them together.

"I'm so proud of you, Ben," Sarah said, her voice filled with warmth. "Your writing is truly remarkable."

Ben's eyes sparkled with gratitude. "Thank you, Sarah. I wouldn't be here without your guidance."

Alex nodded in agreement. "You've made a real difference, Sarah," he said. "You've helped us all find our voices."

Sarah smiled, a sense of fulfillment washing over her. In the tapestry of life's unexpected turns, she had discovered the power of connection, the transformative impact of shared passions, and the enduring beauty of storytelling.

The book launch buzzed with excitement as attendees mingled, discussing the featured anthology and congratulating the published authors. Ben, his youthful face flushed with pride, stood beside Sarah and Alex, basking in the moment of his literary debut.

Suddenly, a familiar voice broke through the chatter. "Ben! There you are! Congratulations!"

A young woman approached them, her smile as bright as the spring sunshine streaming through the venue's windows. It was Maya, Ben's classmate from the creative writing program, with whom he had developed a close friendship.

"Maya, this is Sarah, the editor who helped me with my writing," Ben introduced her, a hint of excitement in his voice. "And this is Alex, my friend and mentor."

Sarah and Maya exchanged warm greetings, and Alex offered a friendly smile. As the conversation flowed, Sarah noticed a spark of something more between Ben and Maya, a shy glance, a lingering touch on the arm.

A bittersweet pang of realization dawned on her. Though happy for Ben's success, she couldn't help but feel a twinge of nostalgia. Their shared journey, fueled by their connection over writing, seemed to be reaching a turning point.

Ben, his attention now drawn to Maya, was no longer the shy freshman seeking guidance. He had blossomed into a confident young writer, ready to embark on a new chapter in his life, both personal and literary.

Sarah excused herself from the conversation, a mixture of emotions swirling within her. She wandered towards a quiet corner of the venue, needing a moment to reflect.

As she gazed at the bustling crowd, a wave of gratitude washed over her. She had witnessed firsthand the power of storytelling, the way it could connect people, inspire dreams, and forge unexpected bonds.

Her relationship with Alex, once filled with intense passion, had transformed into a warm friendship, a testament to the enduring power of shared experiences.

David, her rock and confidant, stood by her side, his unwavering support a constant source of strength. Together, they were building a future filled with love, laughter, and a shared passion for the written word.

The book launch concluded, leaving behind a lingering sense of accomplishment and the promise of new beginnings. Sarah, with Ben's book tucked safely under her arm, stepped out into the cool evening air.

The future stretched before her, an open book waiting to be written. New stories awaited, new connections beckoned, and the power of storytelling continued to weave its magic, shaping lives and creating a tapestry of shared experiences.

Weeks turned into months, and life settled into a comfortable rhythm for Sarah. Her days were filled with the thrill of acquiring new manuscripts, nurturing the careers of budding authors, and collaborating with talented editors at the publishing house.

David continued to be her anchor, their evenings spent in cozy bookstores browsing new releases or curled up on the couch, lost in the worlds conjured by their favorite authors.

One crisp autumn afternoon, Sarah was engrossed in editing a manuscript when a familiar name on the title page caught her eye. It was Alex, listed as the author of a memoir titled "Shattered Illusions: A Journey of Self-Discovery."

A wave of nostalgia washed over her. Memories of their passionate love affair, the tearful confrontations, and the bittersweet reconciliation flooded her mind.

Curiosity piqued, Sarah finished editing her assigned manuscript and set aside some time to delve into Alex's memoir. As she turned the pages, his words painted a vivid picture of his struggles with self-acceptance, his exploration of identity, and the transformative power of advocacy work.

She relived their relationship through his eyes, understanding his perspective with a newfound clarity. The memoir wasn't a recounting of blame or resentment, but rather a story of growth, acceptance, and the enduring power of first love, even in its imperfect form.

Finishing the last page, Sarah wiped away a stray tear. Alex's honesty and vulnerability resonated deeply within her. She felt compelled to reach out, to express her appreciation for his writing and the closure it offered to their shared past.

Picking up her phone, Sarah hesitated for a moment. Then, with a deep breath, she composed a text message: "Alex, just finished your memoir. Beautifully written, honest, and truly inspiring. Thank you for sharing your story."

Hitting send, she felt a sense of peace settle over her. Regardless of how their relationship played out, Alex's story had a profound impact on her life, shaping her journey and reminding her of the importance of self-acceptance

Days turned into weeks, and Sarah received no response from Alex. Though a flicker of disappointment crossed her mind, it quickly faded. The act of reaching out had brought her a sense of closure, a recognition of the past and its lessons learned.

As Chapter 3 draws to a close, the characters stand at a crossroads. Sarah, fulfilled in her career and her relationship with David, embraces the future with a sense of optimism. Ben, with his newfound love for Maya and his blossoming writing career, embarks on a path brimming with possibilities.

Alex, having shared his story with the world, continues his advocacy work, leaving a lasting impact on those navigating their own journeys of self-discovery.

And though their paths may not always intersect, the ripples of change set in motion by their shared experiences continue to reverberate, a testament to the enduring power of storytelling to connect, inspire, and shape the tapestry of our lives.

Time passed slowly, let's go to the next page for further story,

SO LET'S GO.

Chapter 4: New Horizons

Several years had passed since the events of Chapter 3.

SARAH, NOW A SEASONED editor at the publishing house, had established herself as a respected figure in the literary world. Her keen eye for talent and her dedication to nurturing aspiring writers had earned her the admiration of colleagues and authors alike.

Her relationship with David had blossomed into a beautiful love story. They had built a comfortable life together, their evenings filled with laughter, shared dreams, and lively debates about books and the ever-evolving world of publishing.

One sunny afternoon, while browsing the shelves of a local bookstore, Sarah stumbled upon a familiar face. It was Ben, his youthful enthusiasm now tempered with a quiet confidence.

He proudly showed her his recently published novel, a coming-of-age story that resonated with vulnerability and honesty. Sarah beamed with pride, remembering the shy freshman who had sought her guidance years ago.

"Congratulations, Ben! This is amazing," Sarah exclaimed, her voice filled with genuine joy.

Ben grinned, his eyes sparkling with excitement. "Thank you, Sarah. I wouldn't be here without your help. You always believed in me."

They exchanged warm greetings, catching up on each other's lives. Ben shared his experiences navigating the publishing world, the challenges and triumphs of being a writer, and his plans for his next book.

As their conversation flowed, Ben mentioned attending a recent LGBTQ+ advocacy event where he had encountered a familiar face.

"Guess who I saw?" he asked, a hint of intrigue in his voice.

Sarah's curiosity piqued. "Who?"

"Alex," Ben replied. "He was part of a panel discussion about mental health and LGBTQ+ youth. He spoke so passionately about his experiences, and his story really resonated with the audience."

A warm smile touched Sarah's lips. It was gratifying to hear that Alex had found his voice, using his story to inspire and empower others.

A few weeks later, while attending a literary festival, Sarah found herself face-to-face with Alex once again. He was presenting his memoir at a well-attended session, his voice filled with confidence as he spoke about his journey of self-discovery.

After the session, a long line of attendees formed, eager to meet Alex and share their appreciation for his work. Sarah waited patiently, a mix of emotions swirling within her - a sense of closure, a flicker of nostalgia, and a genuine admiration for the person Alex had become.

Finally, it was her turn. Sarah approached Alex, a warm smile on her face.

"Alex," she said, her voice filled with sincerity. "Your memoir was incredibly moving. It brought back a lot of memories."

Alex, his eyes widening in recognition, returned her smile. "Sarah, it's good to see you again. Thank you for your kind words."

They stood there for a moment, a silent understanding passing between them. Their shared past, once a source of heartache, now held a bittersweet tenderness.

"I'm so happy for everything you've accomplished," Sarah continued, her voice genuine. "You're making a real difference."

Alex nodded, a hint of gratitude in his eyes.

"Thank you, Sarah. You too."

They exchanged well wishes, and Sarah turned to leave, a sense of peace settling over her. The encounters with Ben and Alex had brought a sense of closure to their shared past, allowing her to move forward with a heart full of gratitude for the lessons learned and the connections forged.

CONTINUE...

Sarah's encounter with Ben and Alex at the bookstore and literary festival left a lingering warmth in her heart. It was a reminder of the profound impact they had on each other's lives, and how their paths, once intertwined, had diverged yet continued to resonate with a shared past.

Back at the publishing house, Sarah faced a new challenge. The company was undergoing a significant restructuring, with a focus on acquiring digital properties and expanding their online presence. While Sarah embraced the shift towards digital publishing, she worried about the potential impact on her role as a traditional editor, a role she cherished for its focus on the craft of storytelling and the meticulous nurturing of authors' voices.

She decided to champion the importance of literary merit alongside the demands of digital reach. She proposed a new initiative - an imprint dedicated to discovering and publishing high-quality literary fiction, even if they didn't necessarily translate well to the digital format.

David, ever her rock, supported her wholeheartedly. "Go for it, Sarah," he said, his voice filled with encouragement. "Your passion for literature is contagious. You can convince anyone of the value of a good story."

Fueled by his support and her unwavering belief in the power of storytelling, Sarah presented her proposal to the board. The meeting was tense, with some executives skeptical of the viability of a print-focused imprint in a digital age.

Sarah, however, spoke with conviction. She passionately argued that stories, especially well-crafted literary fiction, held the power to transport readers, challenge perspectives, and leave a lasting impact.

"The value of a book goes beyond its format," she declared. "It's about the journey it takes us on, the emotions it evokes, and the way it stays with us long after we turn the last page."

Her words resonated with some board members, particularly those who remembered the enduring legacy of classic literature. After a lengthy discussion, the board approved Sarah's proposal, albeit with a smaller budget than she had initially hoped for.

With unwavering determination, Sarah set about building her new imprint. She scoured through manuscripts, searching for stories that resonated with her, those with powerful narratives and a unique voice.

She discovered a gem - a debut novel by a young writer named Maya, a name that sparked a flicker of recognition. It was Ben's girlfriend, the woman who had captured his heart at the book launch years ago.

Maya's manuscript was a beautifully written coming-of-age story that explored themes of cultural identity, first love, and the complexities of family relationships. Sarah saw a raw talent waiting to be nurtured, a fresh voice that deserved to be heard.

The news that Sarah was considering Maya's work reached Ben first. He was ecstatic, his voice filled with excitement when he called Sarah.

"Sarah, you won't believe it! Maya told me about her manuscript," he exclaimed. "I can't wait for you to read it."

Sarah chuckled, a warm feeling enveloping her. "Believe me, Ben, I already have. And it's fantastic. We're going to make Maya a star."

As Sarah embarked on this new chapter, a sense of satisfaction filled her. Her passion for storytelling had not only shaped her own career but had also given her the opportunity to nurture new talent and champion the power of literature in a rapidly changing world.

The connections she had forged with Ben, Alex, and now Maya became more than just chapters in her personal story. They were testaments to the enduring power of storytelling, a force that could connect lives, inspire dreams, and create a legacy that transcended the boundaries of time and format.

Chapter 5: Echoes of Change

The weight of expectation settled heavily on Sarah's shoulders as she sat down at her desk. Maya's manuscript, a beacon of raw talent, lay open before her. Each word painted a vivid picture, weaving a tapestry of emotions that resonated with a deep honesty. The young writer's potential was undeniable, and Sarah felt a fierce determination to guide Maya's work to its full potential.

This newfound responsibility, however, came with a tinge of pressure. As the champion of Maya's story, Sarah knew her decisions could shape the young writer's career. She meticulously combed through the manuscript, offering constructive criticism and insightful suggestions, all the while nurturing Maya's unique voice.

Across town, David sat hunched over his computer, finalizing his presentation for a major architectural conference. His passion for sustainable design fueled his meticulous attention to detail. Every slide was meticulously crafted, a testament to his innovative ideas for a greener future. Buildings, in his vision, weren't just structures; they were living entities that could seamlessly integrate with the environment, fostering harmony and sustainability.

Despite their demanding careers, Sarah and David found solace in their shared evenings. The weight of the day melted away as they nestled on the couch, lost in the pages of a captivating novel or animatedly discussing their respective pursuits. A silent understanding existed between them, a respect for each other's dreams and a commitment to their shared life.

Meanwhile, in a bustling university classroom, Ben captivated his students with a lecture on the power of storytelling. His journey from a shy freshman seeking guidance to a confident writer had come full circle. He spoke with a passion that resonated deeply with his students, his voice weaving a spell as he encouraged them to find their own voices and weave their unique stories into the tapestry of the world.

Miles away, Alex sat in his office at the community center, reviewing applications for a new youth mentorship program. His journey of self-discovery had propelled him to become a beacon of hope for struggling LGBTQ+ youth. His memoir, a testament to his courage and vulnerability, had become a source of strength for many, a reminder that acceptance and self-love were attainable goals, not distant dreams. As he scanned each application, a sense of purpose filled him. He knew the power of mentorship, the transformative impact of having someone believe in you.

Days turned into weeks as Sarah and Maya embarked on a collaborative journey of editing and refining the manuscript. Sarah's experience and keen eye for detail helped Maya polish her raw talent, while Maya's youthful perspective injected a fresh energy into the process. Their discussions were filled with laughter, thoughtful critiques, and a shared passion for storytelling.

David, ever the supportive partner, took on additional household chores to free up Sarah's time to mentor Maya. He understood the importance of Sarah's role and took pride in her dedication to nurturing new talent. He would often overhear their animated conversations about the book, a smile gracing his lips at Sarah's infectious enthusiasm.

Ben's days were a whirlwind of lectures, student meetings, and working on his own second novel. He found immense satisfaction in inspiring his students, his classroom a vibrant space where creativity flourished. But a part of him missed the camaraderie of writing alongside Sarah and Alex, the late-night sessions fueled by coffee and shared dreams.

One evening, while enjoying a quiet dinner with David, Sarah received a call from the publishing house. Her heart pounded as she listened to the news. The board had greenlit the publication of Maya's book, a decision that filled her with a sense of accomplishment and pride.

Meanwhile, across town, Alex witnessed the positive impact of his mentorship program firsthand. One of his mentees, a young transgender student named Emily, had blossomed under his guidance. Emily, once shy and withdrawn, was now finding her voice, a testament to the power of acceptance and support.

WEEKS BLED INTO MONTHS as Sarah and Maya meticulously polished the manuscript. Maya's raw talent shone through, but self-doubt began to creep in. As publication loomed closer, Maya became increasingly nervous.

"What if it flops?" she confided in Sarah during one of their editing sessions. "What if everyone hates it?"

Sarah squeezed Maya's hand, her voice firm but reassuring. "Don't let those fears hold you back. You've poured your heart and soul into this story, Maya. It's honest, it's moving, and it deserves to be heard."

Despite Sarah's encouragement, Maya's anxiety intensified. Public scrutiny, always a daunting prospect for an author, felt overwhelming for a debutante. Sleepless nights filled with self-deprecating thoughts became a regular occurrence.

The pressure reached a boiling point on the eve of a major book launch event. Maya, overwhelmed by a sudden panic attack, pulled out at the last minute. Sarah frantically searched for her, eventually finding her in a secluded corner of the bookstore, tears streaming down her face.

"I can't do this, Sarah," Maya choked out, her voice trembling. "I'm not good enough."

Sarah knelt beside her, wrapping a comforting arm around her shoulders. "You are good enough, Maya. You have a unique voice, a story that needs to be told. Don't let fear silence you."

A wave of determination washed over Sarah. She wouldn't let Maya's dream crumble under the weight of self-doubt.

"Listen," she said, her voice filled with conviction, "Let's go back. We'll face this together. You wrote this story, and you deserve to stand by it."

Taking a deep breath, Maya wiped away her tears. Sarah's unwavering support instilled a flicker of courage within her.

Arm in arm, they walked back to the event hall. Standing backstage, Maya gripped Sarah's hand tightly, her heartbeat still rapid. But a newfound resolve shone in her eyes.

Sarah squeezed her hand back, offering a reassuring smile. "You got this, Maya," she whispered.

With a deep breath, Maya stepped onto the brightly lit stage, ready to face her fear and share her story with the world.

The End of Chapter 5

This climax section introduces a rising tide of doubt in Maya, a crisis of confidence, and Sarah's unwavering support. It culminates in a turning point where Maya decides to face her fear and share her story at the book launch event. This leaves the reader hanging, eager to know how the event unfolds and whether Maya's book is well-received.

Interval

We will complete this story in volume 2 till then Jai Hind,

stay happy stay safe

About the Author

Mrigendra Bharti, born on June 29, 2004, in South Delhi, India, is a multifaceted individual recognized as the owner of Mrigendra Bharti Group InfoTech India Co. Pvt Ltd. Beyond his entrepreneurial endeavors, he is a distinguished music producer, director, and a budding writer.

Embarking on his professional journey at a young age, Mrigendra Bharti's visionary leadership has led to the establishment of several successful ventures, including Croma Music Series Entertainment, Sellbrochure, Fauget Innovative, and more.

What sets Mrigendra apart is his early initiation into the world of business. His foray into the unknown realms of entrepreneurship began during his 10th-grade years, where he delved into the music industry. This initial venture laid the foundation for subsequent achievements, showcasing his dedication and resilience.

Having honed his skills in music, Mrigendra Bharti not only demonstrated significant growth in his craft but also expanded his professional network. His passion extends beyond music, encompassing app and website development, as well as graphic design.

Fueled by his creative aspirations, Mrigendra established the Mrigendra Bharti Group, a company specializing in website and app development. Currently, he collaborates with a dedicated team, collectively working on ambitious projects that promise innovation and excellence.

Mrigendra's journey serves as an inspiration, particularly for today's students, highlighting the potential of youthful determination and the ability to transform innovative ideas into successful businesses. As he continues to make strides in various domains, Mrigendra Bharti remains a dynamic force, contributing vibrancy to the realms of business, music, and technology.

Read more at https://www.imwriter-mrigendra.rf.gd.